Wolfie's Secret

by Nicola Senior

ff

FABER & FABER

Wolfie was no *ordinary* wolf.
He was a wolf with a SECRET . . .
He was a wolf who loved baking!

Wolfie dreamed of becoming a famous baker.
He fantasised about writing his own cookery books.
He was desperate to have his own TV show.

But everyone knows wolves are meant to be GROWLY, FIERCE and MEAN.

They're not supposed to enjoy icing buns or sprinkling hundreds and thousands on to fairy cakes . . .

So Wolfie was careful to keep his baking a secret.

Wolfie had tried huffing and puffing.
He always *pretended* he wanted to eat grandmas and
little boys and girls! Wolfie even had a checklist to
remind him how wolves are supposed to behave.
Wolfie just wasn't very good at any of it!

1. Act tough

2. Snarl teeth

3. Scare little girls
   and pigs

4. Eat grandmas

Scrumdiddlyun

EAT MORE

Goodies for

One day Wolfie decided to test a new recipe.
He drew his curtains and set to work. He whisked up
the batter; he poured it into the tin; he popped the
cake in the oven.
His kitchen soon filled with a scrumptious aroma.

He hummed happily.

Now, it so happened that there were three little pigs –
Jones, Frank and Marlow – right outside Wolfie's window
at that very moment.

They were looking for a good spot to build a new home.

Jones, the smallest pig, was worried.
'We can't build our house *here*!' he said. 'A wolf lives next
door! He'll surely huff and puff and blow our house down!'

But just as Jones said
these words, the pigs
heard a humming sound . . .
And they smelled something
delicious . . .
CHOCOLATE CAKE!

Everyone knows that chocolate cake is a pig's
FAVOURITE food.
The pigs crept up to Wolfie's window . . . and
they were astonished by what they saw . . .

A wolf in a *pinny*! COOKING!
Why wasn't he sharpening his claws, or huffing and puffing?

'A wolf baking cakes? Whatever next?' squealed
Frank, the oldest pig.

Sewing?

Painting?

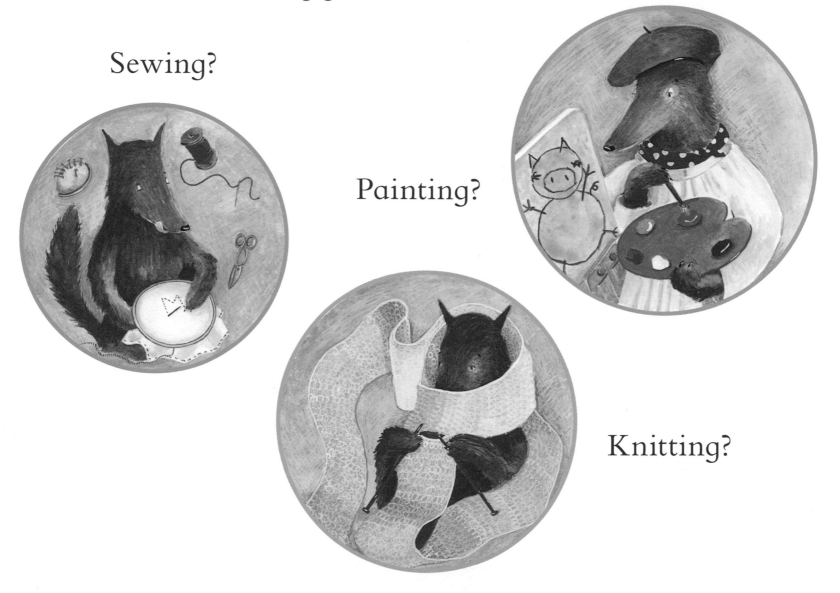

Knitting?

This wasn't how a wolf should behave. Wolfie wasn't
a *proper* wolf. He wasn't scary! The world must know.

The three little pigs started watching Wolfie's every move. They followed him. They took photographs. They noted down his recipes!

Finally they had all the proof they needed.

They took the photographs to the local newspaper . . .

Poor Wolfie had no idea any of this was going on. He'd been too busy creating a recipe for a brand new cake.

The cake was a celebration of grandmas everywhere.

Grandma's Delight

lots and lots of hot buttered toast and tea!

cake and icing and jam and cream!

an oversized hand knitted jumper or two

comfy chair for cuddles

hugs, of course!

So it came as quite a shock when his world was turned upside-down.

THE DAILY TAIL

We are No. 1

EXCLUSIVE
WOLF IN CAKE-
BAKING SCANDAL

FULL STORY INSIDE

Other news:
Public are told:
"Lock your doors,"
as porridge thief
strikes again full story
page 10

It was a Saturday morning. Wolfie had just taken a
batch of fairy cakes out the oven, and was now sitting
enjoying a cup of tea. He picked up the newspaper . . .

. . . and almost choked in shock!

WOLF IN CAKE-BAKING SCANDAL
said the headline! His secret was out!

Wolfie jumped up, closed the curtains
and hid in bed.

The next day, Wolfie didn't even turn on his oven.
He spent the whole day in his armchair, worrying.
Now everyone knew he wasn't a *proper* wolf . . .

Then he heard a funny sound. It was the sound of
something hitting the doormat. Lots of things.

Wolfie trotted to the front door and couldn't believe his eyes. There was an enormous pile of letters on the doormat! He fearfully opened an envelope and began to read . . .

Dear Wolfie,

I am writing to tell you how delicious I found your recipe for scones. All my friends say they are the best I've ever made I've enclosed a picture of them. I wanted to ask if you have any more recipes?

Yours sincerely,

Mr Tooks

Mr. Wolfie
c/o The Daily Tail

newspaper
cakes cakes

Mr. Wolfie
The Baking

ing wolf
The Daily Tail

The letter congratulated him on being an excellent baker! He opened up another, and another: every single letter was full of praise for him. At the bottom of the pile was a large brown envelope.

Dear Mr Wolf,

I want to apologise for exposing you as a cake-baking fraud. It was very unkind of us to do that without your permission and I am sorry for the upset we caused.

I also wanted to write to you because we have been inundated with letters from our readers. They want more recipes! If you could forgive us, I would like to offer you a job writing a weekly recipe column for the newspaper.

Yours hopefully

Mr P. Encil (editor)

Wolfie was amazed. No one was laughing at him. They all admired him!

Just as he thought the day couldn't get any better, there was a knock at the door. In front of him were three little pigs, looking rather sheepish.

'We have a present for you,' said Marlow.

'It's a cake mixer,' said Jones.
'So you can bake more easily,'
finished Frank.

Wolfie didn't know what to say . . .
but he knew exactly what to do!
He invited the three pigs inside.

FLOU

Scones

Everybody loves scones
and everyone has their
very favourite way of
eating them. How do
you like to eat yours?

with
butter

or

jam and
cream?

Wolfie showed Marlow
how to crack an egg.

He helped Frank
cream the butter.

He let Jones stir in
the milk.

Ding went the oven.

The scones were ready!

And the happy baking wolf and the three little pigs
sat down for a lovely tea.

THE END

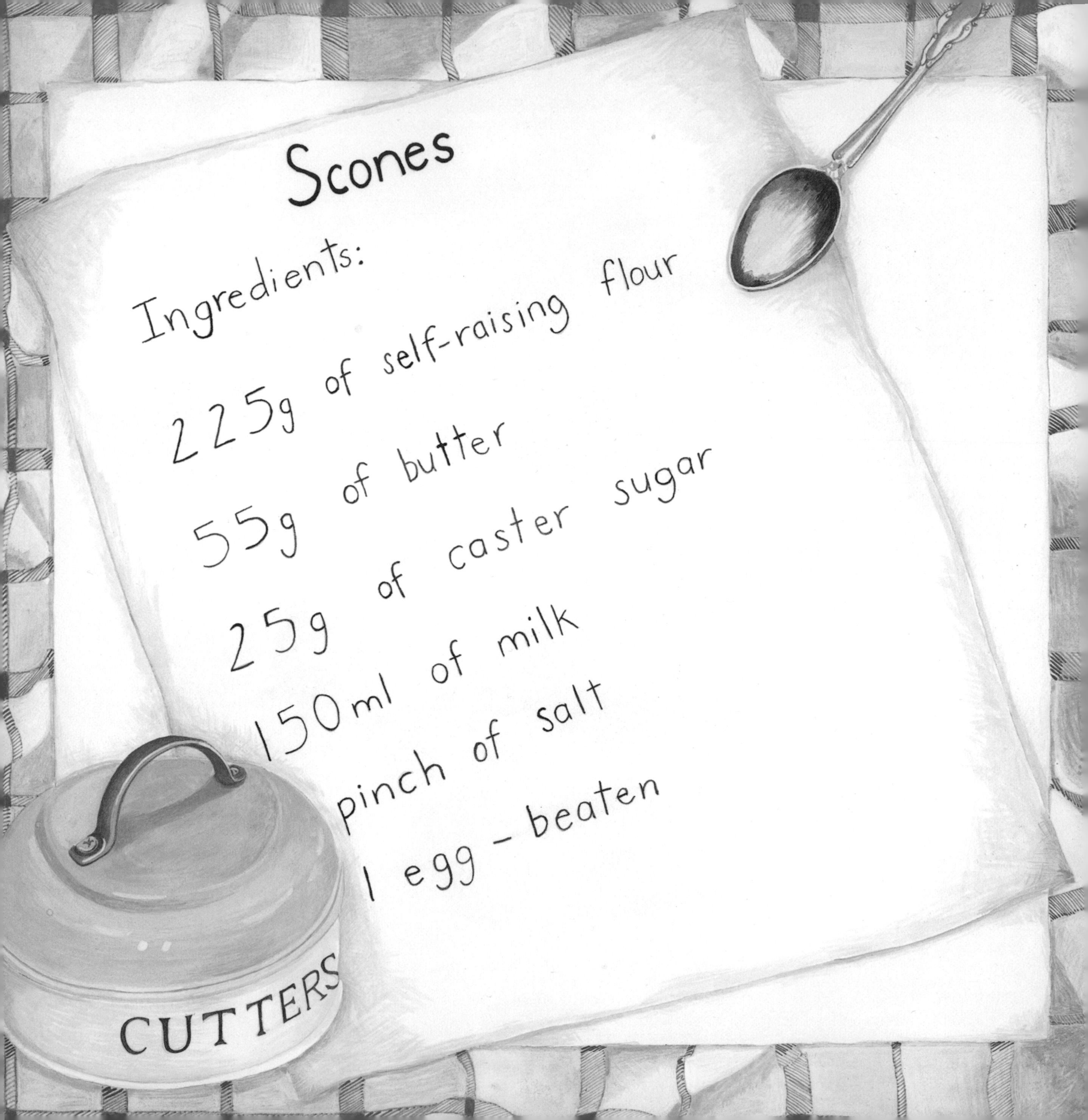

Scones

Ingredients:

225g of self-raising flour

55g of butter

25g of caster sugar

150ml of milk

pinch of salt

1 egg – beaten

CUTTERS

- Preheat the oven to 220°c and wash your hands!

- Grease a baking tray

- Mix together the flour and the salt and rub in the butter

- Stir in the sugar and the milk to get a soft dough

- Knead lightly (if you have furry paws this is where it gets sticky!)

- Pat the dough out into a 2cm round

- Cut out the scones with a 5cm cutter

- Brush the tops with beaten egg

- Bake for 12-15 mins

- Once cool spread with butter (or cream and jam)

- Scrummy scrummy, eat and enjoy!

FLOUR

SUGAR